WALT DISNEY

Cinderella

ILLUSTRATIONS BY THE WALT DISNEY STUDIO

ADAPTED BY CAMPBELL GRANT

FROM THE WALT DISNEY MOTION PICTURE "CINDERELLA"

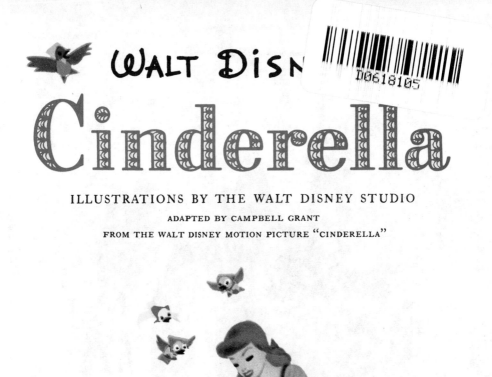

gb GOLDEN PRESS

Western Publishing Company, Inc.

Racine, Wisconsin

This Little Golden Book was produced under the supervision of

THE WALT DISNEY STUDIO

The Little Golden Books here bring you, in gay color, delightful stories and illustrations adapted from the world-famous Walt Disney Motion Pictures. In them you will find Pinocchio, The Three Little Pigs, Bambi, Dumbo, Uncle Remus, Cinderella, Alice in Wonderland, Peter Pan, and many other well-loved Disney characters.

Thirty-Seventh Printing, 1980

Copyright MCML by Walt Disney Productions.
World rights reserved.
Produced in U.S.A. by Western Publishing Company, Inc.

ONCE UPON A TIME in a far-away land lived a sweet
and pretty girl named Cinderella. She made her home
with her mean old stepmother and her two stepsisters,
and they made her do all the work in the house.

Cinderella cooked and baked. She cleaned and scrubbed. She had no time left for parties and fun.

But one day an invitation came from the palace of the king.

A great ball was to be given for the prince of the land. And every young girl in the kingdom was invited.

"How nice!" thought Cinderella. "I am invited, too."

But her mean stepsisters never thought of her. They thought only of themselves, of course. They had all sorts of jobs for Cinderella to do.

"Wash this slip. Press this dress. Curl my hair. Find my fan."

They both kept shouting, as fast as they could speak.

"But I must get ready myself. I'm going, too," said Cinderella.

"You!" they hooted. "The Prince's ball for you?"

And they kept her busy all day long. She worked in the morning, while her stepsisters slept. She worked all afternoon, while they bathed and dressed. And in the evening she had to help them put on the finishing touches for the ball. She had not one minute to think of herself.

Soon the coach was ready at the door. The ugly stepsisters were powdered, pressed, and curled. But there stood Cinderella in her workaday rags.

"Why, Cinderella!" said the stepsisters. "You're not dressed for the ball."

"No," said Cinderella. "I guess I cannot go."

Poor Cinderella sat weeping in the garden.
Suddenly a little old woman with a sweet, kind face
stood before her. It was her fairy godmother.

"Hurry, child!" she said. "You are going to the ball!"

Cinderella could hardly believe her eyes! The fairy
godmother turned a fat pumpkin into a splendid coach.
Next her pet mice became horses, and her dog a fine
footman. The barn horse was turned into a coachman.

"There, my dear," said the fairy godmother. "Now into the coach with you, and off to the ball you go."

"But my dress—" said Cinderella.

"Lovely, my dear," the fairy godmother began. Then she really looked at Cinderella's rags.

"Oh, good heavens," she said. "You can never go in that." She waved her magic wand.

"*Salaga doola,*
Menchicka boola,
Bibbidy bobbidy boo!" she said.

There stood Cinderella in the loveliest ball dress that ever was. And on her feet were tiny glass slippers!

"Oh," cried Cinderella. "How can I ever thank you?"

"Just have a wonderful time at the ball, my dear," said her fairy godmother. "But remember, this magic lasts only until midnight. At the stroke of midnight, the spell will be broken. And everything will be as it was before."

"I will remember," said Cinderella. "It is more than
I ever dreamed of."

Then into the magic coach she stepped, and was
whirled away to the ball.

And such a ball! The king's palace was ablaze with lights. There was music and laughter. And every lady in the land was dressed in her beautiful best.

But Cinderella was the loveliest of them all. The prince never left her side, all evening long. They danced every dance. They had supper side by side. And they happily smiled into each other's eyes.

But all at once the clock began to strike midnight, Bong Bong Bong—

"Oh!" cried Cinderella. "I almost forgot!"

And without a word, away she ran, out of the ball-room and down the palace stairs. She lost one glass slipper. But she could not stop.

Into her magic coach she stepped, and away it rolled. But as the clock stopped striking, the coach disappeared. And no one knew where she had gone.

Next morning all the kingdom was filled with the
news. The Grand Duke was going from house to
house, with a small glass slipper in his hand. For the
prince had said he would marry no one but the girl who
could wear that tiny shoe.

Every girl in the land tried hard to put it on. The
ugly stepsisters tried hardest of all. But not a one could
wear the glass shoe.

And where was Cinderella? Locked in her room.
For the mean old stepmother was taking no chances of
letting her try on the slipper. Poor Cinderella! It looked
as if the Grand Duke would surely pass her by.

But her little friends the mice got the stepmother's key. And they pushed it under Cinderella's door. So down the long stairs she came, as the Duke was just about to leave.

"Please!" cried Cinderella. "Please let me try."

And of course the slipper fitted, since it was her very own.

That was all the Duke needed. Now his long search was done. And so Cinderella became the prince's bride, and lived happily ever after — and the little pet mice lived in the palace and were happy ever after, too.